Being Friends

For a free color catalog describing Gareth Stevens' list of high-quality books and multimedia programs, call 1-800-542-2595 (USA) or 1-800-461-9120 (Canada). Gareth Stevens Publishing's Fax: (414) 225-0377. See our catalog, too, on the World Wide Web: http://gsinc.com

The author and original publisher would like to thank the staff and pupils of the following schools for their help in the making of this book: St. Barnabas Church of England Primary School, Pimlico; Kenmont Primary School, Hammersmith & Fulham; St. Vincent de Paul Roman Catholic School, Westminster; Mayfield Primary School, Cambridge; St. Peter's Church of England School, Sible Hedingham.

Library of Congress Cataloging-in-Publication Data

Althea.
    Being friends / by Althea Braithwaite; photographs by Charlie Best; illustrations by Conny Jude.
        p. cm. — (Exploring emotions)
    Includes bibliographical references and index.
    Summary: Examines the nature and value of friendship and how it can have its ups and downs.
    ISBN 0-8368-2115-7 (lib. bdg.)
    1. Friendship in children—Juvenile literature. [1. Friendship.]
I. Best, Charlie, ill. II. Jude, Conny, ill. III. Title. IV. Series: Althea. Exploring emotions.
BF723.F68A57   1998
177'.62—dc21   98-5587

This North American edition first published in 1998 by
Gareth Stevens Publishing
1555 North RiverCenter Drive, Suite 201
Milwaukee, Wisconsin 53212 USA

This U.S. edition © 1998 by Gareth Stevens, Inc.
First published in 1997 by A & C Black (Publishers) Limited,
35 Bedford Row, London WC1R 4JH. Text © 1997 by Althea Braithwaite.
Photographs © 1997 by Charlie Best. Illustrations © 1997 by Conny Jude.
Additional end matter © 1998 by Gareth Stevens, Inc.

Series consultant: Dr. Dorothy Rowe

Gareth Stevens series editor: Dorothy L. Gibbs
Editorial assistant: Diane Laska

Printed in Mexico

1 2 3 4 5 6 7 8 9 02 01 00 99 98

Exploring Emotions

Being Friends

Althea

**Photographs by
Charlie Best**

*Illustrations by
Conny Jude*

17999

Gareth Stevens Publishing
MILWAUKEE

What is a friend?

A friend is a person you trust, someone you care about and who cares about you.

Friends put up with you when you are grumpy or moody.

My friends make me laugh.

4

Friends understand you. You can tell them anything.

How do you show someone you are a friend?

Our friends may be very different from each other. Some friends are full of energy and are lots of fun.

I like Tom. He makes me laugh. He never stops talking!

Other friends are easy to talk to about problems.

Rubia is much quieter than Tom. She listens to me.

Some people prefer a large group of friends. They think it's important to like many people, and they want many people to like them. They might even worry if they think someone doesn't like them.

Other people are happier with one or two close friends.
They don't worry so much about how many
other people like them.

You might get angry and argue with a best friend, but you probably won't stay angry very long, because you care so much about each other.

We didn't speak to each other for a week, but, now, we're best friends again.

11

Family members can be friends, too. Even brothers and sisters who find it hard to like each other all the time can usually count on each other for support when they are sad or need help.

They hug me when I'm feeling miserable.

Do you have any grown-up friends? Sometimes a person much older than yourself is very easy to talk to.

Zoe says, "My mom has a friend who is very good about helping me with my problems. When she comes to stay with us, I talk to her a lot."

Getting together with
a group of friends
can be a lot of
fun. Belonging
to a group
can make you
feel good.

Sometimes, however, people do things in a group that they wouldn't do alone. For instance, a group might ignore someone and not let that person play with them. Groups sometimes tease or bully a person who is alone.

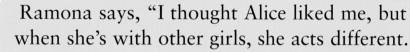

Ramona says, "I thought Alice liked me, but when she's with other girls, she acts different. Sometimes, she picks on me."

They call you "chicken" if you don't do what they say.

15

As you get older, the way you feel about people and things probably will change. Even best friends can change.

"I went away on vacation last summer and, when I came back, Paul was best friends with someone else. I think he was jealous that I got to go on a trip."

It can hurt when a close friend makes friends with someone else, but it doesn't always mean that the two of you have to stop being friends.

I felt jealous when Zoe made friends with Alice, but, now, the three of us are friends.

Sometimes, people need time alone. Being alone doesn't mean a person is lonely; he or she just might need to be alone for a while. When do you like to spend time alone?

Peter says, "I like writing stories and painting pictures, but I need to be by myself to really concentrate on them. I don't want to spend all my time with other people, not even my friends."

"I didn't stop liking my best friend, but I needed to spend some time with other people, too. He was a little upset at first, but we still play together."

Making friends can be difficult. Sometimes,
people feel lonely and left out when
they see other people enjoying
themselves together.

*I wish
I could play.*

Perhaps they haven't noticed
that there are other people
who feel lonely, too. Those
people might welcome the
chance to make friends, even
if they're too shy to say so.

When you're trying to make new friends, it's not always best to choose the most popular children. Getting to know them well might be difficult if they already have many friends.

Do you know anyone who does things just to be liked?

Anna's always showing off because she wants to be popular.

We don't have to be friends with everyone. We can choose who we like and who we don't. We're all different, and we can't expect to like and be liked by everyone.

22

Some people have difficulty making friends because they think other people won't like them.

When we learn to like ourselves, other people are more likely to care about us, too.

We might not always understand our friends, but that doesn't stop us from liking them.

We can learn a lot about someone by being his or her friend.

Getting to know a person as a friend can teach us a lot about ourselves, too. For example, if we don't care how our friends look, we might not worry so much about how we look.

Whether we are close to one person or many people, friends help us gain more confidence to be ourselves.

25

For Teachers and Parents
A Note from Dorothy Rowe

We make and lose friends throughout our lives, so teachers and parents know that children frequently will experience problems with friendships. Adults sometimes forget, however, that, in order to help, they first must find out how the child sees the problem.

A child won't see a situation the same way an adult does for the simple reason that no two people, whatever their ages, ever see things in exactly the same way. An adult shouldn't assume he or she knows what's wrong with a child but, rather, should explore possible reasons for the child's behavior by seeking answers to questions like: "Does this child have difficulty making friends?" or "Is this a child who would prefer to have one good friend instead of many friends?"

Dozens of reasons are possible answers to the question, "Why does this child behave this way?" Thinking of these alternatives helps the adult ask better questions. The answers, however, can come only from the child.

The expectations people have of friendships can differ considerably. Adults must be prepared to share with children their own experiences, including the difficulties they have had dealing with friendships. They should not pretend to provide easy solutions to the problems that children encounter in making and being friends. This way, adults and children can explore the joys and complications of friendships together.

Suggestions for Discussion

To start a discussion and get everyone involved, have the children help you compile a list of qualities that are significant in friendships. Then have them rank these qualities in order of importance to them. In comparing their answers, the children can discuss why they feel certain qualities are the most important in a friend.

Some examples of the expectations and qualities of friendship are:

- A friend is someone you can trust, someone who will keep your secrets and won't tell them to other people.

- A friend puts up with you even when you are in a bad mood.

- A friend sticks up for you when other people are being mean to you.

- A friend doesn't gossip, speak unkindly, or tell lies about you behind your back.

Many aspects and complications of friendships and how to deal with them can be discussed with children while going through this book, page by page. The following points might help start your discussions.

Pages 6-7
Some people are willing to be your friend when everything is going well for you, but they don't support you when you need comfort or help. These people sometimes are called "fair-weather friends."

Pages 8-9
Because people are individuals, they can be quite different from one another. Not everyone you want to be your friend will choose you as a friend. In the same way, you will not choose everyone who wants to be your friend. Choosing how many friends you want and who they will be is up to you. Try not to let other people's opinions control your choices.

Page 10
Some friends might have difficulties greater than having to wear glasses or being the shortest person in class. It takes courage to stick up for them when they are being picked on or teased.

Page 11
In what different ways do children make up after arguments? If an argument develops into a feud, making up can become very difficult.

Page 13
A child might develop friendships with people other than children of his or her own age for a variety of reasons.

Page 15
Sometimes, children do things when they are part of a group, or want to be, that are wrong or that they normally would be ashamed to do.

Pages 16-17
What does it feel like to be jealous of someone? What has made you jealous of people in the past?

Pages 18-19
When people need time alone, their friends should not feel neglected or insulted.

Page 20

Some people make friends easily. Others worry so much about themselves and their own feelings that they don't notice the people around them who need and want their friendship.

Page 22

People might behave in unusual ways when they want to be noticed. How can this kind of behavior sometimes be harmful?

Page 23

New situations can be scary, but you can do a lot of things to help new people feel welcome. Try not to judge people by the way they behave at first, because they sometimes act differently if they are scared or shy.

Pages 24-25

Friendships don't happen instantly or automatically. They develop as people get to know each other, and they depend on people being honest about who they are.

More Books to Read

Best Friends. Hope Benton (Open Minds)

Emotional Ups and Downs. Good Health Guides (series). Enid Fisher (Gareth Stevens)

Ernestine and Amanda. Sandra Belton (Simon and Schuster Children's)

Friendly. Feelings (series). Janine Amos (Raintree Steck-Vaughn)

Friends Indeed. Lois M. Wright (Vantage)

Give and Take. Jim Boulden and Joan Boulden (Boulden Publishing)

Sticks. Joan Bauer (Delacorte)

Videos to Watch

Being a Friend: What Does It Mean? (Sunburst Communications)

Being Friends. (Rainbow Educational Media)

Let's Be Friends. (Sunburst Communications)

Let's Get Along (series). (United Learning, Inc.)

Web Sites to Visit

KidsHealth.org/kid/feeling/

www.pbs.org/adventures/

Due to the dynamic nature of the Internet, some web sites stay current longer than others. To find additional web sites, use a reliable search engine with one or more of the following keywords to help you locate information about being friends. Keywords: *behavior, emotions, feelings, friends, friendship, pals, relationships.*

Glossary

argue — to disagree verbally, sometimes in an irritated or angry way; to quarrel.

belonging — accepted as a member of a group or a set of people.

bully — a person who makes a habit of being mean or cruel to others, especially those who are weaker in some way.

confidence — faith and trust in the value of your character or abilities, or in the character or abilities of another person.

friend — a person who has affection and respect for another person; a favorite companion.

ignore — to pay no attention; to turn away from on purpose.

jealous — feeling hostile toward someone who has things or advantages that you think should be yours.

lonely — feeling left out and sad about being alone.

popular — well-liked; accepted by almost everybody.

show off — to behave in a special or unusual way for the purpose of attracting attention.

shy — tending to withdraw or stay away from other people.

support — help, encouragement, comfort, or guidance from another person or source.

tease — to annoy or irritate someone in a mischievous way.

trust — to believe in and depend on the strengths, character, and honesty of another person.

understand — to recognize, accept, and care about the circumstances of another person.

Index